After school, Blake and I walked home together. We had walked home together every day since kindergarten. But for some reason I was having trouble talking to him. I pointed out the pink and white cherry blossoms that had just appeared, and tried to act natural. Inside, I was feeling anything but natural.

We walked along in silence for most of the way. I thought that Blake might have been feeling a little uncomfortable, too.

Finally, he said, "See you in 30 minutes to go over to the rec center." Then he disappeared into his house.

I smiled all the way home. I felt so funny. It had always been easy to share my innermost feelings with Blake. But now, when we talked, I felt scared and happy at the same time. It was a weird sensation.

THE GREAT Boyfriend Disaster

By Cindy Savage

To Ardis
without whose support
I wouldn't get anything done.

Cover photo by John Strange

Published by Willowisp Press, Inc.
401 E. Wilson Bridge Road, Worthington, Ohio 43085

Printed in the United States of America

10 9 8 7 6 5 4 3 2 1

ISBN 0-87406-240-3

One

I crunched on a tortilla chip. "Your turn," I informed Blake.

"Come on, Suzanne. Just give me some time," he said, grinning. "This one little letter of the alphabet has the power to break my neck."

I tapped my pencil on the paper where a drawing of a stick figure hanging in a noose stared back at me. "Go ahead. Guess," I teased. "The gallows await."

Blake's forehead wrinkled. He glared at me across our favorite picnic table under an oak tree in the center of the school lawn. "It's not fair," he said. "You knew this word was impossible to get before we even started. I give up."

I smiled. "You're not going to get out of it that easily."

"Okay, okay. *U*. Is it *u*?" he guessed.

"Sorry, but you weren't even close," I said, drawing the final foot on the doomed hangman. "The word was *gendarme*. It means *soldier*. We learned it in history class today."

"Like I said, it's not fair. I don't have history till last period." Blake tried to pout, but he couldn't hold back a smile. "I should never play hangman with you, Suzanne. Your vocabulary passed mine at age three." He laid his head on the table in a mock faint.

Before I could say anything more, some of the rest of our regular lunch group arrived. "Is he dead or alive, Suz?" Tang greeted us loudly.

"Dead," I said, shaking my head sadly. I lifted Blake's limp hand and let it fall back onto the table.

"Well, dead or alive, move over anyway," Tang said, giving Blake a shove. "We need room for the trays."

Tang is the crazy one of our group. His real name is Terrence. But we started calling him Tang in kindergarten, because he always arrived at school with an orange mustache from drinking Tang orange drink at breakfast. His hair has about a hundred cowlicks. It stands straight up whether that's the style or not. He's a whiz at word games, and no matter what he says, he always has a punch line.

Blake rolled his head and flopped back against the tree, continuing his dead act. Blake is a little strange, too. He doesn't look crazy like Tang. In fact, I personally think he's kind of cute with his sad, blue eyes and flyaway brown hair. But, he has a way of acting serious when he's really kidding that fools most people. He doesn't fool me, though. I've known him too long.

"Okay, Blake, you'd better come back to life," Tiffany, my second-best friend next to Blake, admonished, shaking her finger at Blake's closed eyes. "Or Suzanne will have to give you mouth-to-mouth resuscitation."

I couldn't believe she'd said that.

Fortunately, Joyce and Mac showed up, carrying their lunch trays, before I had time to get really embarrassed. Joyce is my other best friend.

"Gosh, by the time we get through the line, lunch period is almost over," Joyce complained, slipping onto the picnic table bench.

Mac slid in beside her. "We ought to brown-bag it like Suzanne and Blake. Think how much more time we'd have!"

"Speaking of time," Blake interrupted, suddenly coming to life, "if we're going to enter the Anything That Floats race, we'd better start spending a few hours after school at the recreation center."

We spent the next few minutes discussing the guidelines for the race that's sponsored each year by a local restaurant called The Brass Fishhook. Individuals or groups can enter. The rafts must be original designs, and they have to float down the river for one mile. The race course starts near the recreation center and ends at the restaurant. The first contestants to arrive with their raft still in one piece win free dinners each month for a year.

Actually, almost everyone wins something. The Brass Fishhook makes sure of that. They have prizes for the strangest, the funniest, the fastest, the most colorful, even the first raft to sink. You have to be 13 to enter the competition. So even though our gang had watched and cheered the race for years, this was the first time we'd been old enough to participate.

"Anybody have any ideas for the design?" Blake asked.

"How about a windmill with little American flags flapping from every blade?" Tang suggested.

"Too top-heavy," said Mac. "How about an old-fashioned log raft?"

"Too dull," I broke in. "What if we get a couple of pontoons, put a bicycle on top, and make a paddle wheeler?"

Joyce stood up. "The trouble is, we need something really original. Something no one has ever done. Something so spectacular that people will be talking about it for years to come!" In her enthusiasm, Joyce waved her hands and knocked over her milk.

We all jumped up, trying to avoid the flood. "Nice going, Joyce," Mac said.

"Quick, get my books," Tiffany yelled. "It's coming this way."

Blake started humming the theme music from *Jaws*, while Joyce ran to get paper towels.

"Joyce is right," Blake said after we'd finally mopped up the table. "We need to do some serious planning. How about if we meet at the rec center after school and discuss our ideas?"

The bell rang as we agreed. Blake tapped my shoulder as I was turning to leave. "See you after school," he said.

"I'll meet you out front as usual," I replied.

I joined Tiffany and Joyce, and the three of us headed for the gym. We're all in a special modern dance class instead of regular phys ed. Lately, we've been working on routines for the eighth-grade graduation assembly.

We changed into our leotards and leg warmers, then did our individual warm-ups. Ms. Masera put on a cassette, and the class spread out to stretch in unison to the music.

Ms. Masera clapped for our attention when the song ended. "I expect to see rough walk-throughs of your ideas for the assembly by the end of class today," she said. Tiff, Joyce, and I walked over to the corner of the room to practice in private.

I jumped up and twirled around in a circle.

"Is that supposed to be part of the routine?" Joyce asked with a giggle.

"Maybe," I said. "I feel great today." I danced around a little more. I kept thinking about Blake. We'd been friends all our lives. But ever since last week's school dance, my feelings for him had been different.

"What's the matter with you, Suz?" Tiff asked. "You have the weirdest look on your face."

"Maybe she ate something strange at lunch and she's going to be sick," Joyce teased.

"Speaking of sick," I said, "I could have killed you for that mouth-to-mouth resuscitation remark at lunch today." But before I could get an apology out of Joyce, Ms. Masera showed up.

"All right, girls, let's get to work," Ms. Masera said as she joined our group. "What do you have so far?"

The three of us lined up with Tiffany in

front and Joyce and I to each side of her and a little behind. We showed Ms. Masera what we'd worked out. I thought we did pretty well, considering we hadn't practiced very much.

"Nice," she told us, and then proceeded to show us how we could make a movement crisper here and change a hand position there. "I really like the feeling you've put into the steps. Keep up the good work."

Ms. Masera left us to go watch another group, and my mind drifted back to Blake.

"She's doing it again," I heard Joyce whisper.

"Earth to Suzanne," Tiffany said, giving me a little shove on the arm. "What is wrong with you today?"

"She's had that look ever since the dance last week," Joyce said.

"You know, you're right," Tiffany agreed.

"Come on, you two," I said, pulling my thoughts away from Blake. "We want this to be the best routine in the program," I added, trying to be serious. But the three of us broke into a bad case of the giggles.

Two

AFTER school, Blake and I walked home together. We had walked home together every day since kindergarten. But for some reason I was having trouble talking to him. I pointed out the pink and white cherry blossoms that had just appeared, and tried to act natural. Inside, I was feeling anything but natural.

We walked along in silence for most of the way. I thought that Blake might have been feeling a little uncomfortable, too.

Finally, he said, "See you in 30 minutes to go over to the center." Then he disappeared into his house.

I smiled all the way home. I felt so funny. It had always been easy to share my innermost feelings with Blake. But now, when we talked, I felt scared and happy at the same time. It was a weird sensation.

* * * * *

On the way to the rec center that afternoon, I had come up with a really great idea for our float entry. But I was having trouble drawing it or putting it into words. Blake seemed to understand what I meant, but he couldn't draw it either.

I ripped a sheet off the pad and started over. "I'm talking about a large, prehistoric animal with wings. You know, like a pterodactyl," I told the group, trying to outline the shape with my hands and my pencil.

"But, Suzanne," Tang interrupted, "pterodactyls flew. They didn't swim."

"But they dove into the water for their prey. And that's what I mean. We could rig the neck some way so the beak could dip below the water and bring up a fish with the name of the restaurant on it. That would catch everybody's attention."

"But wouldn't the neck and head tip the raft over when it bent down?" Tiffany asked with concern. "Otherwise, I really like the idea. No one has done a dinosaur before. Maybe we'd even get our picture in the paper, or win the prize for most original."

"I know there is a way to do it." I sat back and stared at my sketch. It looked more like something my two-year-old sister, Carolyn, would do. "I can't help it if I'm not an artist. Why don't we go talk to Sam. Maybe he'll have something in his salvage yard that we can use to support the thing."

Thinking that was a reasonable idea, we all trudged out the back door of the center and headed across the field to Sam's Salvage and Surplus.

Sam told us to have a look and see what we could find. So we wandered through the piles of old machinery, used car parts, wire spools, and factory containers. We had been coming here all our lives, just to see what treasures we could find.

Blake and I had built our first fort out of boards and cardboard tubes from Sam's. We had fixed our bikes with salvaged parts and found the tires that formed the ladder steps to our tree house there. Sam's salvaged treasures always fired my imagination.

"Look at this long plastic pipe." I lifted the length of it and tested the weight. "It's not too heavy. Maybe we could use it to support the dinosaur's neck. And, look over there," I said, running to the spot. "This green cellophane stuff would make great scales."

"Here's more cellophane," Tiff called from the other side of the stack. "Maybe there's enough to cover the whole beast."

Everybody jumped into the act, yanking out rolls of almost brand-new green cellophane. "This is great!" Mac said excitedly.

Tang was uncovering something in another pile. Mac went over to help him. "Look at this, guys," Mac shouted. "An old pontoon boat. I'll bet we could patch these holes and the pontoons would still float."

"What a find!" Tang said. "This will make a perfect base for our float. Don't you think so, Blake?"

Blake shook his head as if to clear it. "What? Oh . . . sorry, I wasn't listening."

"Is something on your mind, Blake? You've been kind of out of it ever since you picked me up at my house," I said. "What's wrong?"

He stuck his hands in his pockets and kicked a can. "Aw, my parents have some old school buddies moving back to town with two kids, Tom and Andy. The kids have been away at some fancy private school. Mom told me I have to show Andy around, introduce him to my friends."

"How old are the kids?" Mac asked.

"Andy's 13, like us. Tom is a junior in high school, so he must be 16 or 17."

"What's wrong with that?" Tiffany asked. "We could use a few extra hands on the float, and we'll all help you show him around at school."

"It's just that I have better things to do than baby-sit a rich, boarding-school kid," Blake said. "He probably thinks he's better than the rest of us anyway."

"You don't know that. He might be nice," I added. "When are they moving in?"

"This weekend." He sighed, clearly not that excited about the idea.

"That's only two days away," Joyce informed us. "Why don't you bring him to the center on Saturday afternoon, and we'll make some cookies to welcome him."

Blake smiled and came over to help me pull on a stubborn piece of green plastic. "Thanks, you guys. In case you couldn't tell, I wasn't too thrilled about the idea."

"Naw," Mac said, shaking his head. "No one could tell."

* * * * *

Saturday dawned bright and clear, promising to be a beautiful April day. The birds woke me up early, so I had plenty of time to bake chocolate chip cookies for Andy's welcoming party.

I was a little surprised that Blake hadn't

called last night to tell me about Andy and his family. But I assumed that with dinner and getting acquainted and all, he probably hadn't had time.

Humming, I wrapped the cookies in foil. Carolyn toddled into the kitchen. "Su Zu, tookie," she said.

"Yes, I made cookies." I picked her up. "But you have to eat breakfast first," I told her.

She smiled and showed me a cut on her finger. It had been there for days, but she was still very interested in it. "Owie," she said very seriously.

I kissed her finger and put her in the high chair.

Just then my father entered the kitchen, sniffing the cookie smell and smiling at Carolyn's raised finger. "Still trying to get a little more mileage out of that owie, aren't you, sweetie?" He bent down and kissed her finger.

He eyed the foil-wrapped cookies. "Any left for me?" he asked.

I grinned. "Good morning, Daddy. Yes, I saved some for your lunch." I pointed to a few unwrapped cookies still on the cooling rack.

"Mmmm," he said, sniffing. "How about one for breakfast?"

"You're a terrible example for Carolyn," Mom teased as she came into the kitchen and caught Dad with a cookie. "What got you up so early this morning?" she asked, turning to me.

"The birds, actually. I'm going to the rec center to work on the raft. We finally think we have a way to make the head of the dinosaur go up and down without tipping over."

We talked more about the race while we ate breakfast. Then Mom asked what the cookies were for.

"Blake's parents have some friends moving back to town after living on the East Coast for the last 10 years. Their son Andy is our age, and Blake is bringing him to the center to help us with the raft. We're going to have a welcome-back-to-Arizona party for him."

"Sounds like fun," Mom remarked. "More fun than I'm going to have. I have to go shopping." She wrinkled her nose in distaste. Mom hates shopping. She says it's faster to make a whole dress than to find one she likes in the store.

"Well, have a good day," Dad said. "I'm off to work," he added, grabbing his coat off the rack in the corner. Normally my father didn't work on weekends, but a big shipment came in for his office supply store, and he was going in for a few hours to get things organized.

"Mom, would it help if I took Carolyn to the

center with me? She could play while we work," I said, holding Carolyn up to wave to Dad through the kitchen window.

"No thanks, honey. Myra Tucker owes me a couple of hours of baby-sitting. I'm going to take Carolyn over there. Are you sure you don't want to go shopping with me?"

"I don't think so. Maybe next time."

"That polite answer doesn't fool me. You hate shopping more than I do."

"I'm my mother's daughter," I quipped.

Three

COOKIES in hand, I headed for the recreation center. Tiffany, Joyce, and Mac were already there, and Tang arrived shortly after I did.

Tiffany handed us each a pair of scissors and a pattern for the dinosaur scales. We set to work tracing and cutting the hundreds of cellophane scales we would need to cover the outside of our beast.

"My dad says we can borrow his aluminum boat for a base if we want," Joyce offered.

"I thought the rafts had to be made from scratch," Tiffany said.

"I think Tiffany's right," I interjected. "They don't want anyone to have an unfair advantage. Besides, we're probably going to need a wider base than a boat to hold up the dinosaur head."

"Oh, that reminds me. I brought a surprise."

Tang jumped up and jogged over to a large plastic garbage bag he had come in with. "I thought this might make a good head for old dino."

He pulled a large papier-mâché creation out of the bag. It looked like a cross between a piñata and a Chinese New Year dragon. He grinned. "Like it?"

"Uh-hum." Mac cleared his throat. "It's a bit large, don't you think?"

"But noticeable from a long way off," Tang countered.

"Definitely noticeable," I said, warming up to the idea. "Would you mind if we cut off a few streamers and repainted it?" I walked over to get a better look.

"Not at all. My sister had to wear this in a play for her fourth-grade class. She said if I didn't want it, she was just going to throw it away."

"Throwing it away sounds like a good plan," Tiffany mumbled under her breath.

I had to disagree. "It's not that bad, Tiff. With a few changes, we could make it work. Let me just climb up on the ladder and see what it looks like on top of the pipe."

From the top of the ladder I had a good view of all the other teams working on their float projects at the center. Another group of middle school students was working on a log raft. I was glad we'd decided against that idea. A group of high school kids was creating something that resembled an airplane.

I placed the dragon head on top of the pipe, then leaned back to look at it. "The streamers will definitely have to go," I announced.

"Rip them off," Tang yelled up at me.

"You don't have to yell. I'm not up that high."

Our group all started to talk at once. "A little to the left." "Squeeze the nose out a bit." "Can you tip it down some?" "Do we really want that thing?"

Suddenly it got quiet. I adjusted the huge head one more time, then looked down to see what everybody thought. "How's that?" I asked as I turned and noticed that they were all staring at Blake and a tall, blond girl.

I looked behind them to spot Andy, but all I saw was Blake's grinning face, and the girl with the gorgeous hair.

"Where's Andy?" I asked from the top of the ladder.

"Believe it or not, this is Andy. *Andy* is short for *Andrea*," he said with a puppy-dog smile.

Joyce was the first to recover from the shock. "Hi. We thought you were a boy," she said. "That's why we're all standing around with our mouths open. I'm Joyce. This is Tiffany, Mac, and Tang. And up there on the ladder is Suzanne."

"Hi," I said and gave a little wave. I couldn't stop looking at her. She was beautiful.

"Don't worry about the name mix-up. People always think Andy is a boy's name until they meet me," she reassured us.

"No one makes that mistake once they meet her, though," Blake added unnecessarily.

"Hi," she called up to me. "Blake's been telling me all about you, Suzanne. I'm glad to finally meet you."

"Yeah, same here, *Andy*." I stressed the boyish sound of her name. It was the only thing boyish about her. She looked as if she could have walked off the cover of *Seventeen*. But it wasn't her looks that bothered me. It was the way she was touching Blake's arm. Her long, polished fingernails stood out against his blue shirt.

She took her hand away in the same casual manner she had laid it there in the first place. I breathed a sigh of relief as she turned her charm on Tang.

"What can I do to help?" she cooed. Her voice was soft, almost a whisper. She made a show of folding up her sleeves, cuff by cuff.

She leaned over the pile of scale cutouts beside Tang. Her hair swished around to brush his face. "I came to work," she added with a smile.

Right, I thought. *She came to work on getting a boyfriend.* I sneaked a glance at Tiffany. She rolled her eyes and went back to cutting scales. Joyce walked over to hand Andy a pair of scissors and a length of green cellophane.

"I hear you went to private school before moving back here. How did you like it?" I heard Joyce ask as Andy took the scissors.

"It was okay, I guess," she said seriously, then turned a warm smile on Blake and Tang. "But we didn't have boys, and we never did anything as neat as this."

If she hadn't been around boys, where had she learned all her moves? She was keeping everyone so busy with her hair-swishing and eye-batting that no one even noticed I was still up on the ladder.

Instinctively I reached up and touched my fluffy bob. Last week Blake had said he liked my new haircut, but after seeing Andrea's tumbling, blond curls, I wondered what had possessed me to cut my own waist-length locks. It was obvious that Blake was really taken by Andy's appearance.

Finally, Blake left the group and climbed a

few steps up the ladder to greet me. He was still wearing the grin he had on when he walked through the door.

"Hi," he said. "Want to join us on the floor?"

"I don't know," I replied, trying not to listen to the musical sound of Andy's laugh. "The view up here is good."

In a flash, Blake climbed up and perched one rung below me. "You're right. Hey, nice surprise, huh?" he said, waving his hand toward Andy. "My mouth practically dropped open when the Irwins came over last night and introduced their *daughter*."

"It hasn't closed yet, I see." The retort just popped out.

But Blake didn't hear me. He was still looking down at Andrea.

"I'm glad she turned out to be nice," he said. "Her stories about girls' school life are so funny. I was expecting to be bored silly taking a boarding-school snob on a tour of Parker, but Andy's so excited about everything, she made it fun."

"I'll bet!" I muttered, wondering just how *fun* their tour had been.

"What?"

"We're all set," I said. I had to remind myself that Blake didn't know how my feelings toward him had changed. "How do you like the pterodactyl's head?"

"It looks more like a dragon," Blake responded, climbing down off the ladder. "What do you think, Andy?"

"Oh, I thought it *was* a dragon. I'm sorry. But that head and these green scales—I just assumed it was a dragon."

"Hey, why don't we change it into a flying dragon instead of a dinosaur?" Blake suggested. "Then the head won't have to tip down into the water. What do you say, Suz?"

What I thought was, *She's only been here 10 minutes and she's already after my boyfriend and my project.* What I said was, "It's up to the group."

We took a vote and decided to change the float. I clenched my teeth and cut out 100 scales in less than five minutes. All the while I listened to Andy making more sweet suggestions in a helpless-sounding voice.

"I don't understand," Mac finally said. "Can you draw us a picture?"

"Well, I'm not a very good artist," she said softly. "But I'll try."

I laughed to myself. Let her try. I tried all afternoon yesterday and couldn't get it right.

But Andy did. In a few minutes she drew a perfect flying dragon—wings, scales, and all. It was just as I had imagined it, but it came out of her pen. My heart sank.

"Wow, we really needed you on our team," Tang exclaimed. "Now I understand what Suzanne was trying to get at the other day. Maybe I can even rig up something to make the wings flap up and down."

His excitement was contagious. Soon the ideas for improvements were flying. In the midst of it all, Andy spoke up. "I'm really glad Blake introduced me to all of you. I know I'm going to like it here, if I ever learn to find my way around."

"Oh, we'll be happy to assist you in any way we can," Tang offered. This statement was met with agreement by everyone.

Everyone except me, that is. I wandered away to get a drink from the water fountain and visit the other groups. For some reason, I just didn't want to be around the gang right then. I was afraid I might cry.

Four

THE next week at school was terrible. Andy went everywhere with us. She was in several of my classes, and she ate lunch with us. It didn't take a genius to notice how the boys hung on her every word.

And what was worse, Blake barely said two words to me. He spent most of his time talking to Andy. Each day I pounded out my frustrations in modern dance class, trying to exhaust myself into forgetting the way he looked at her.

"Why don't you talk to him?" Tiffany suggested after I told her that I hadn't seen Blake for days, except when we were working at the center.

"I know he'll tell me he's only spending so much time with Andy because his parents told him to show her around. He called one evening, and all we talked about was how Andy was having such a hard time adjusting to public school. He said he was trying to help her out. Poor little Andrea. I almost slammed the phone down in his ear."

"Give her a chance, Suzanne. Andy seems nice enough, and everyone appears to like her," Tiffany said.

"So if she's not having a hard time adjusting and making friends, why does she need so much help from Blake?"

Tiffany shook her head and changed the subject. "We'd better get to class. Rumor has it that Mr. Boxwell has a pairs project to assign today. I hate it when they break us into pairs. I always get stuck with Malcolm Morton."

Pairs, I thought happily as we entered the room. I felt sorry for Tiffany. But for me pairs were great. Suzanne Doyle and Blake Franklin. Boxwell uses alphabetical order for everything, and that will put Blake and me together. I smiled as I slid into my seat in the second row.

"Fancy seeing you here," Blake whispered from behind me. "How was your weekend? Want to go early to the center this afternoon and stop by the ice-cream shop?"

I turned and flashed him a wide smile. Maybe things were okay after all. Ice-cream stops were our normal afternoon routine. I faced front again just as Mr. Boxwell, or Boxy, as everyone called him, rapped his yardstick on the desk for attention.

"No one can keep a secret around here," he said in a deep disapproving voice. "So, as many of you already know, we're going to do a partners project. It will include both a written and an oral report, which both partners must write and present equally."

A chorus of groans rose in the room. I looked over at Andy in the next row. She looked terrified.

"This will be something new for all of you," he was saying. "For this project, you will be required to get married, get a job, and have children."

He paused to wait for our response, which wasn't long in coming.

"How long is this project supposed to take?" Tang called out from the back row. "We only have four more weeks of eighth grade." The class burst into laughter.

"I knew you were going to ask that," Boxy continued. "You'll have two weeks to complete the assignment, and then we'll take the last two weeks of school for the oral presentations."

More groans followed that announcement,

but I was excited. Blake and I would have to spend a lot of time together. With a little luck, maybe Andy would get interested in her new "husband" and leave Blake alone.

I glanced over at her out of the corner of my eye without turning my head. She really did look scared. *Maybe she gets panicked doing oral reports,* I thought.

"It's very convenient," Mr. Boxwell went on, "that we have an equal number of boys and girls in this class. I've matched you up in couples using alphabetical lists. Prepare yourselves to meet your future husband or wife."

"Mary Adams and John Booth, Roxanne Bixby and Jamie Calzon," Boxy read, checking off the pairs. "Karen Cades and Leroy Dacker, Suzanne Doyle and Terrence Dalmas, Andrea Irwin and Blake Franklin, Charlotte Johnson and . . ."

I didn't hear any more. It finally occurred to me that the new guy, Leroy, had messed up the order.

This time when I looked over at Andy, she was smiling at Blake. All traces of terror were gone from her face. I listened as Boxy droned on with the assignments. The only nice thing that occurred was that Tiffany managed to get paired with Mike instead of Malcolm. I was happy for her.

My mood sank even lower when Boxy set himself up as Justice of the Peace in front of the class and started marrying the couples. I had to watch Andrea and Blake exchange fake wedding vows. Then I had to stand up there with Tang and pretend to be enjoying myself.

"Well, if nothing else," someone shouted from the audience. "Marriage with the big T ought to be a lot of laughs."

"Hey, cheer up," Tang said as we took our seats. "I promise to love, honor, and do the dishes."

"Laundry, too?" I asked, cracking a small smile. It was hard to stay mad for long when Tang was around.

"So long as you take care of the dirty diapers," he bargained.

"No thanks. I do enough of that at home."

"All right," he agreed, throwing up his hands. "We'll get a kid that doesn't poop."

"Speaking of kids," Boxy said when the laughter finally died down, "you don't get a choice as to how many you'll have. And you don't get to choose your own careers. I have 15 envelopes with life plans in this basket. I want each pair to pick an envelope on the way out."

He walked to the front of each row and handed the first person in each row a stack of papers. "Pass these back. These are your assignments. Taking into consideration your particular life plan, each couple must write out a budget and a report on what you do on a daily basis—who takes care of your children when you are at work, who takes care of them if you travel for business, etc. I want a detailed list of the pros and cons of your situation. I know you can't move into each other's houses, but I want you in contact all the time. If you don't have your partner's phone number, get that right now. Congratulations, newlyweds, and good luck!"

I shuffled out of the room next to Tang, who insisted on holding onto my arm. "She's a little weak after the excitement of the ceremony," Tang told Boxy as he grabbed for an envelope. "Does this one look all right to you, sweetheart?"

"Can I sue for divorce?" I pleaded with Mr. Boxwell.

"Only after your two weeks are up," Boxy replied with a chuckle. "In fact, that's one of the questions on the assignment sheet. *Number 16: Do you want to stay married to this person?*"

Tang put his arm around me, and kissed the air by my ear with a loud smack. "Let's not talk of divorce, dear. We haven't had our honeymoon yet." He offered his arm. "May I escort you to lunch, Mrs. Dalmas?"

"Forget calling me Mrs. Dalmas," I exclaimed, pushing my way out the door. "I'm keeping my maiden name."

As funny as the situation was, I couldn't stop thinking about Blake and Andy walking right behind us. She'd probably love to take his name.

"Hey, wait up!" Tiffany called, running to catch up with us. "Let's read our life plans over lunch. I can't wait to see what Boxy has in store for Mike and me."

"Where is Mike? I thought we were supposed to stick to our partners like glue for the next two weeks," I said, staring at Tang until he dropped my arm. "Is there trouble in paradise already?"

"No. Mike had band practice. He said he'd call me tonight."

We talked about the project throughout lunch. Tiffany read her life plan aloud. "We're both commercial airline pilots. Well, that's convenient," she said with a giggle.

"Only if you work for the same airline," Tang broke in.

"That's true," Tiff agreed, then continued scanning her paper in silence.

"What does ours say?" Blake asked Andy.

She made a great show of opening the

envelope. Then she passed it to Blake, and with an overly sweet voice said, "You read it, dear."

I almost gagged.

"Get on with it," Tiffany prompted, looking up from her reading. "We only have 30 minutes for lunch."

Andy sighed as Blake began reading. "We both have college degrees, and we own a chain of fast food franchises."

"Hey, what a coincidence. Isn't that almost what your parents do now?" Joyce asked.

Andy nodded, then resumed listening to Blake.

"We have two children, a boy and a girl, who go to the best private schools. We have a house in the suburbs and a condo in the mountains."

"Oooh, the perfect couple!" Tiffany exclaimed. "You're lucky. It should take you about five minutes to complete your report. Ours says Mike will lose his job two days after we find out that I'm pregnant. We'll have to cope with big medical bills and no money."

"Mr. Boxwell doesn't mention any problems in our plans," Blake said, waving the paper.

"Well, then, we'll just have to think of some way to spend all that money." Andy batted her eyelashes at Blake. "How about a cruise to the

Carribbean? Australia? Or, we could just take a cruise around the world."

"How about a weekend in Disneyland? We still have to work you know," Blake reminded her.

"Aye, aye, captain." She jumped up, saluting. "Maybe we should let our friends help us decide."

The group delighted in giving Blake and Andrea a list of ways to spend their fortune.

I finally raised my voice above the others. "But even perfect couples have problems," I said sweetly. "The two of you will probably get stressed out trying to maintain such a high life-style. Then you'll have to go to therapy. Blake will have a heart attack from work overload, and your kids will get into trouble at school because they don't get enough love at home."

"Sad, but true," Tang said, raising his napkin to his eyes. "What was once a happy home is now an empty shell." He sniffed loudly and pretended to blow his nose into the napkin.

I didn't notice that Andy was the only one not laughing until after my final punch. "You might even beat Tang and me to the divorce courts."

Five

I ended up walking over to the center by myself that afternoon. Andy's mom had picked up Blake and Andy after school to go house-hunting with the Irwins. I couldn't see why it was so important that Blake go along. After all, it was the Irwins who had to live in the place, not Blake.

With each step I took, I remembered how angry I'd been when Mrs. Irwin had arrived to surprise them. It made me especially upset when Blake crawled into the backseat with Tom to let Andy have the front with her mother and father. But instead of taking the seat he'd offered so politely, Andy squeezed in right beside Blake. Then she had the nerve to wave to Tang and me as they drove off.

By the time I got to the center I had calmed down a bit. Actually, I had begun to think that Blake's going along on the house hunt was a good thing after all. The faster Andrea Irwin's family found a place to live, the faster she would move out of the Franklins' spare bedroom. *Maybe the Irwins would even move out of the school district, and Andy would have to transfer,* I thought gleefully.

Humming, I entered the rec center to find Tang up on top of the ladder, painting fangs on Dino, our dragon.

"He's supposed to be a friendly beast," I said, laughing up at Tang. "We don't want to scare the judges away."

"Don't worry, wife-o-mine, he'll be friendly. Friendly, and hungry."

"For fish," Mac said, waving a large cardboard cutout of a fish with *The Brass Fishhook* printed across one side of the belly and *Sam's Salvage and Surplus* on the other. Sam had given us all the supplies for free, so we wanted to put in a plug for him.

The float was beginning to take shape. The large, green dragon head was attached to a long plastic pipe that was covered with hundreds of shimmery green scales. Tang had rigged up a wooden box that held the neck and wings in place. We had bolted the whole contraption to a plywood base and propped it up against a wall to keep it from falling over.

"All we need now is a tail as long and heavy

as the neck to balance the thing. Then we'll be all set."

"Shall we go back to Sam's for another pipe?" I asked just as Blake and the everpresent Andy showed up.

We all discussed the tail problem for a few minutes. Then Andy said, "Why not make Dino's tail out of chicken wire and papier-mâché? That way we'd get the shape we want."

"But it would be too light," I said smugly.

"We could fill the tail with rocks or sand to make the weights match," she flipped back without even looking at me.

"Great idea, Andy," Blake said, patting her on the back. He got his hand tangled in her hair, and they spent about five minutes goofing around trying to get it out.

I had just about had it. All my earlier calm was gone. I walked over to the table and picked up a pair of scissors. Smiling mischievously, I turned and asked, "Need some help?" I snipped the scissors opened and closed.

Andy's eyes widened. Blake miraculously freed his hand from her curls. Then he walked over to me, took the scissors, and placed them on the table. "What's your problem?" he asked.

"Nothing."

Turning back to the table, I quickly set out paper cups and opened the thermos of iced tea my mom had sent over. "Refreshments, anyone?" I handed a glass to Blake. Joyce came up to take a cup, and so did Tang and Mac. Tiffany picked up one for herself and held one out to Andy just as I turned to do the same thing.

My arm bumped Tiff's, dumping the full glass of iced tea down the front of Andy's shirt. She screamed.

"Oh, gosh, I'm sorry," Tiffany and I both said at once. I grabbed a paper towel and started to dab at the wet shirt.

"Give it here!" Andy ordered, taking the towel from me. "You're just spreading it. I'll have to go into the bathroom and wash it out."

"Good idea," I said.

"Come on, I'll go with you," Tiffany offered. She gave me a look like she thought I'd done it on purpose.

I really hadn't, but I guess everyone thought I had. I looked up to find the whole group staring at me. Quicky, I avoided their eyes and began mopping up the floor with the rest of the paper towels.

"That was a really dumb stunt," Blake finally said.

"I didn't do it on purpose, Blake Franklin! Tiff and I just bumped cups, that's all."

"Sure, and you weren't going to cut off Andy's hair, either?"

"Of course not," I said, standing to face him squarely. "I was joking." I decided to go on the attack. "I suppose your hand was *really* stuck in Andy's hair for five minutes?"

"As it so happens, it was."

"Right!"

"My ring got stuck."

"It's never got stuck in my hair," I countered.

"There's a first time for everything," he replied.

We were standing nose to nose now, fighting just as if we were little kids again.

"Hey, hey, hey, children." Tang pushed his way between us. "Fight later. Right now we have work to do. Here comes Tiffany. Let's get busy."

"Is Andy all right?" Blake asked Tiff.

Tiffany looked back and forth between us. "Sure, she's fine. The tea didn't leave a stain. She's just waiting for the hand blower to dry her blouse."

I hid a smile. It might have been an accident, but I really wasn't sorry.

"Tang's right. I think we'd better get back to

work," Mac spoke up. He and Joyce began gluing scales onto the box.

When Andy came out of the rest room, Blake went over to her. I could hear him apologizing again for my behavior, but I didn't bother to correct him. What was the use? If he wanted to think I had spilled my drink on purpose, let him.

"We're going over to my house to rustle up some chicken wire and newspapers," Blake called to the group. He didn't even bother to say good-bye to me.

A few minutes later Tiffany joined me to work on covering the wings. They were made out of two layers of old paneling that Mac's dad had taken down from his den. Mac had cut them out with a jigsaw, using a pattern that Andy had drawn. They looked great. Sandwiched in between the two halves was a metal bar, which Tang had attached to the pedals and chain drive of an old bicycle. When the pedals turned, the wings raised and lowered like they were flapping in the wind.

Our entry was really beginning to take shape. But I was too upset with Blake to get excited about it.

"Coming to my house for our regular sleepover tonight?" Tiffany asked. "My mom made six different kinds of hors d'oeuvres for us to sample. She's catering a wedding in a few weeks, so we get to try out some new recipes for her."

"Okay," I said, perking up a bit. "Who's coming?"

"You, me, and Joyce. Who else?"

"Oh, I thought you might have invited Andy." I tried to sound as if it didn't matter whether she had or hadn't.

"I did invite her, but she couldn't come. Her family has plans to do something tonight."

"Oh," I said, trying not to sound too happy.

"You really should give her a chance, Suzanne. She's nice once you get to know her."

I changed the subject before I said something I would regret. "Do you want me to bring the game tonight? Dad's been teaching us this new card game called Zip Zap. It takes four decks."

"Sure. It sounds fun. I'll ask Joyce to bring the chips and something to wash down the hors d'oeuvres."

I laughed. "I have to leave early on Saturday morning," I told her. "Tang and I are getting together to work on our social studies project before we meet back here. We have to find a baby-sitter for our six kids."

"Bring them along. We could use the extra help."

Six

"THAT was a good game," Joyce said, pushing back from the card table and patting her stomach. "Good food, too."

The three of us had demolished the whole tray of snacks Tiff's mother had prepared, and were halfway through the chips and dip.

"Those little pizza roll-ups were terrific. But I think I ate too many. Why don't we take Buffy for a walk around the block? I need some exercise."

"Great idea," Tiff said. "Then we can come back and sit in the hot tub for a while."

We all agreed. Joyce and I cleaned up our mess while Tiff found the dog leash. She called Buffy, and a second later the Maxwell's Great Dane skidded into the kitchen. As a puppy, this behavior was cute. As a 150-pound dog, it was just short of disastrous.

"Buffy, calm down," Tiffany ordered. "Sit!"

Buffy sat—right on my foot.

Fortunately it only took Tiffany a second to hook the leash onto Buffy's collar, so I was saved hospitalization for a crushed instep.

"Sorry, Suzanne," she said when she saw me rubbing my foot. "Buffy thinks she's still a baby."

"A baby horse," I retorted.

Buffy eagerly led us toward the front door. Just as we got there, the doorbell rang.

"You made it after all," Tiffany greeted Andy. "Great! Drop your bag in the entry hall. We're taking Buffy for a walk. How did you manage to get away?"

"My parents canceled our plans tonight to have a talk with my older brother. They didn't need me around, so I talked them into letting me come here." Andy smiled and said hello to the rest of us. "Oooh, what a neat dog," she squealed.

"Watch out!" I warned her. "He's an attack dog."

"Don't believe a word she says, Andy. Buffy is as gentle as a kitten."

"A kitten named Moose," I said, pushing past them out the door. "Are we going to take a walk, or stand around gabbing all night?"

Buffy chose that moment to charge past me. "I guess we're going for a walk." Tiffany laughed as she let the dog yank her along.

Outside, the air was still. A hint of a cool breeze caused a flutter in the treetops.

"Want to talk about it?" Joyce asked. We had fallen behind Tiffany and Andy, who were still trying to keep up with Buffy.

"I think I need to change my image," I said, an idea coming to me.

"But you look fine the way you are. In fact, I wish I looked half as good as you do."

"I'm sorry I cut my hair."

"I love your new haircut. Hey, does this have anything to do with Andy?"

"Blake seems to like how she looks. I have to do something. We used to at least be friends. Now he barely knows I exist."

"Well, if you want to know what I think . . ."

"Shhh, we're catching up with them." Tiffany had a firm hold on Buffy's leash to slow the dog down.

"Are you telling secrets about us?" Tiffany joked.

"We're just talking about new looks," Joyce covered.

"What did you have in mind?" Andy asked, warming quickly to the subject. "New clothes? New face?"

Tiff and Joyce laughed, but I was serious. "Maybe, but I have barely 10 dollars saved up from my allowance. I was thinking more along the lines of makeup."

"Hey, I know," Tiffany said. "My mom has a whole drawer of makeup she doesn't use. The colors aren't right for her. She said I could borrow from it any time I want. That's where I got this great blusher."

I looked at her face and couldn't see any trace of makeup on her cheeks. "What blusher?"

"Okay, so I don't trust myself to put on very much."

"What did you do? Wave the brush near your face and hope?"

"Honest, I really did put some on this morning," Tiffany said defensively.

"You do a good job with your makeup," Tiff continued, turning to Andy. "Maybe you could give us some tips."

"Yeah, that's a great idea," Joyce chimed in.

"I'd love to," Andy said excitedly.

We took Buffy home and spent the next few hours changing from glamorous to gloppy. We changed our hair. We tried different cheek, lip, and eye colors. We got so involved that I almost forgot Andy was there—almost.

"I can't seem to get this blush on right," Joyce complained. "I look like a clown."

"Here, let me show you," Andy offered. She

and Joyce giggled as Andy demonstrated where the blusher should go.

"Where did you learn all this stuff?" Tiff asked her.

"Oh, the Academy had a special arrangement with a modeling school. They taught us how to use makeup, how to walk and sit—all that stuff," Andy told her.

"Tell us about the Academy," Joyce said. "You hardly ever talk about it."

"There isn't much to tell. It was just a school, kindergarten through twelfth." She went back to outlining her eyes with blue pencil.

"But Blake said you had a lot of stories about private school life and traveling overseas," Tiffany insisted.

"She doesn't want to talk about it. Let it drop," I interrupted. I was tired of Andy's fairy-tale life dominating the conversation.

"Oh, that's okay. I don't mind," Andy spoke up. "Well, there was this one time when the seventh-grade girls locked the door to the teacher's lounge, and . . ."

Tiffany and Joyce leaned forward to catch every word. I turned back to the mirror to concentrate on curling my hair. *Let her talk,* I thought. *I don't care. So what if Joyce and Tiff are traitors? Just when you think your friends are loyal, they turn on you. Who needs them?* I tried to convince myself.

"This is the new me that I like best," I exclaimed as I surveyed myself in the full-length mirror on the back of Tiffany's closet door. My hair was curled on top. I had on peach blush, coral-tinted lip gloss, brown mascara, and beige and brown eye shadow.

"What do you think?" I asked my friends and Andy. I had to admit she knew what she was doing, even if I didn't like her.

Joyce flipped her ponytail out of her eyes and looked at me carefully. "You look good, Suzanne. You look like a slightly less pale version of your regular self."

I smiled. "That's just the effect I was hoping for. You, on the other hand, look like something Buffy dragged in. What is that glittery stuff on your cheek?"

Joyce stood up and spun around. Her ponytail circled the top of her head like a helicopter. "This is my rock-star look," she said, posing with an imaginary guitar across her middle.

"You look great." Tiffany complimented Joyce over her shoulder in the mirror on her dresser. "No one would even recognize you. You should go to school like that and freak the teachers out."

"Unfortunately, the first person to get freaked would be my mother. I'd never get out the front door."

"What do you think of this look?" Tiffany turned around, and Joyce and I both gasped at once.

"You look just like your mother!" we said at the same time. Tiffany had pinned her hair up into a French twist in the back and pulled a few wisps of bangs down in the front. The resemblance was amazing.

"My goodness! Am I looking into a mirror?" Mrs. M exclaimed from the doorway. "Gosh, I didn't know I was so gorgeous."

We all laughed.

"I didn't realize how much I look like you until I did this," Tiffany said, looking at her reflection again.

"I came in to tell you that it's midnight," Mrs. Maxwell said, smiling. "I thought I heard Suzanne say she had to go home early tomorrow."

"You're right. Thanks for reminding me. I guess we'd better forget the hot tub."

"By the way girls, take anything you want from that drawer. It's just going to waste in there."

"Thank you, Mrs. M," we called after her as she headed down the hall to her bedroom. We cleaned our faces and each chose a few makeup samples to take home.

I put my new treasures in my purse. I couldn't wait to see Blake's face when he caught a look at the new me. *Watch out, Andy,* I thought.

As I drifted off to sleep, a plan formed in my mind for how to win Blake back. I decided to try the first act out on Tang the next day.

Seven

TIFFANY, Joyce, and Andy were still asleep when I woke up the next morning. I gathered my stuff and said good-bye to Tiffany's mom. Then I took my bike out of the garage and rode the three blocks home.

I greeted my parents in the dining room, and raced to the bathroom to put the first part of my plan into action. I did my makeup just the way I'd done it at Tiff's house. It took me 10 minutes to transform myself into the "new" Suzanne. I searched through my closet for something other than jeans and a sweatshirt to wear, but all I found was the dress I'd worn as a bridesmaid in my cousin's wedding and a skirt that was three years old and totally out of style. I hated to think about it, but it looked like I'd have to go shopping.

I settled on a fairly new shirt that I hadn't worn much and a pair of newer jeans. I walked back into the kitchen, and knew by the surprised look on my parents' faces that they had noticed the new me.

"My, Suzanne you look . . ." Dad began.

"Nice," my mom supplied.

"I was going to say older," Dad continued.

I smiled at both compliments and thanked them.

"I thought I'd try something new," I told them. "I'm tired of looking like a boy."

"You never looked like a boy to me," Dad said, grinning.

"Dads are supposed to say that." I turned and popped two slices of wheat bread into the toaster and waited for them to toast. After putting peanut butter on one and jelly on the other, I sat down across the table from Mom and Dad.

I took a bite of the peanut butter toast. "Mom, could we go shopping this afternoon? I'd like to get a skirt."

Mom almost choked on her hot chocolate. "You actually *want* to go shopping? Wait a minute. A skirt? Is the choir performing at school or something?"

I took a bite of the jelly toast. "No, I just need some new things. Everything I have is a wreck. As much as I hate to say it, it's time for me to go shopping."

"This is a job for you, John," Mom told Dad. "A birthday gift here, a pair of jeans there. Those things I can handle. But updating an entire wardrobe is beyond my tolerance level."

Dad put down his paper and took a long look at the new me. "Yes," he said. "I think it's time you had a few new things. And, as unusual as it is around this house, I enjoy shopping."

"Thanks, Daddy. Is tomorrow okay?"

"How about tonight?"

"Tonight's great. Tang's coming over this morning, and we have to work on the raft at the center this afternoon. But this evening I'm free."

"It's a date then. After dinner we'll hit the mall."

The doorbell rang.

"That must be Tang. I'll get it," I announced with a little too much eagerness.

Mom rolled her eyes at Dad. I was sure they couldn't understand why I had made myself all up for Tang when I know they suspected I liked Blake. I didn't understand either, exactly, but it had something to do with trying to show Blake that I could get along without him. I wanted to show him that the time he spent with Andy didn't matter. Then I wanted him to apologize to me.

"Hi, Tang. Come on in."

Tang noticed the new me right away. "What's all that yuck on your face?" he asked.

"Thanks a lot, Terrence. I can see I really impressed you."

"Oh, you impressed me all right. Or should I say, you made an impression."

"You don't like my new look," I said as I led him through the living room.

"I didn't say I don't like it. I'm just not used to you looking so sophisticated, that's all."

"Do you think Blake will like it?"

"Oh! So, that's what your new image is all about. And, here I thought it was because you married me." He stuck his lower lip out in a pout.

I threw my hands in the air. "I give up! I can't please anyone. And don't you dare start analyzing *that* statement."

We sat down at the table. "Are we having our first fight, sweetheart?" Tang asked. "We'd better write this bit of marital history down in our notes."

"Who has time to fight? Have you read our data sheet? We have six kids, you just lost your job, and I have to go back to work to support the family. Hey, that means we'll get to decide what jobs we'll have," I said. "We have to develop a budget, a child care plan, and a list of possible complications and solutions."

"I can think of one problem right away. I'm going to have to look for a new job immediately, because I'll go crazy if I have to stay home and take care of six runny-nosed brats," Tang said.

"Well, if you do that, we'll need day-care when the kids aren't in school. Or else you'll have to do your job-hunting when the kids are in school, and plan to be home by the time they get home."

"How old are these kids anyway?" Tang asked. "Can't some of them be in college so I won't have to cook for an army?"

"Are you planning to cook?" I asked incredulously.

"It's the least I can do if you're out working all day."

I held up my hand. "Hang on. I'm writing all this down. I think we should write this like a journal or diary, so Mr. Boxwell can see that we've planned out every minute of our lives."

For the next half hour we made up names and ages for our imaginary kids. We figured out what grades they were in and what times they were in school. Then we decided that I would get a high-powered position in advertising for a big agency. My job would make Tang feel even worse about losing his job.

"Yes, I can see where you getting a great job after years at home raising kids would make me feel inadequate," Tang admitted. "Let's say I got laid off when the computer firm where I was vice president changed ownership. That way, losing my job would be no disgrace. But it would be hard for me to find a similar position, because I'd be so overqualified."

"That's good, very good," I commented, writing as fast as I could. "In fact, why don't you decide to start your own consulting firm. That way, we'd have another whole list of problems concerning the start-up of a new business."

"I should know about that. That's just what my father did. For a while he was working 20 hours a day. We never saw him. But, now his business is going strong, and he's around more. He even went to my brother's Little League game yesterday afternoon."

"You know, our data sheet is actually making it easier to come up with problems and solutions than some of the others we heard," I said.

"You're right," Tang agreed. "Look at Blake and Andy's situation. They start out with the perfect family, income—everything. Then they have to create problems. I think that way would be a lot harder than starting with the problems and working toward the solutions."

"Maybe so," I admitted. "But I'm sure Andy will figure out a way to keep them working on their project day and night for the whole two weeks."

"You're sounding jealous again," Tang warned, laughing. "Andy's not so bad. She's just new and needs a few friends."

"Andy needs support. Andy needs friends." I threw down my pen and shoved my chair back from the table. "Andy has you all fooled into believing she's helpless. I don't think she's helpless at all."

Tang just shrugged.

Eight

I had to admit that the chicken wire and papier-mâché creation that was now Dino's tail looked pretty good. Even though Tang and I were late, Blake and Andy weren't there when we arrived at the center. I was disappointed that I couldn't make the spectacular entrance I'd planned.

Mac didn't even notice my new look. He was too busy looking at Joyce's swinging ponytail. Tiffany had gone back to being her usual self.

I started to work right away, gluing scales on the lower part of the tail. "When did you guys attach this?" I asked. I thought I'd been at all the work sessions.

"Blake came in early this morning and hooked it on. He left a note."

Eagerly I unfolded the piece of paper. It read, *We have to take the Irwins out house-hunting again this morning, so I came in early to put on Dino's tail. I hope to see you guys later this afternoon.*

"Sorry all your image-changing went for nothing," Tang said when he saw the expression on my face. "I guess Blake isn't coming after all?"

"Who cares whether he comes or not?" I snapped. "Besides, I didn't change my appearance for him. I did it for me!"

"Whatever you say, wifey-poo."

"Anyway, Blake said he'd try to make it in later. But don't get the idea that I care one way or the other."

The afternoon dragged on as I glued scales on Dino. I was so upset with Blake and Andy that I kept making mistakes and globbing glue all over everything.

Suddenly, two hands covered my eyes. "Guess who?" a mumbled voice whispered in my ear.

Instantly my mood changed. "Blake," I almost shouted. I turned to face him, glancing around behind him at the same time. "Where's Andy?" I ventured.

"They found a house to rent, and she's helping with the move."

"Well, that's super!" I said with a little too much excitement. "I mean, I'm sure the Irwins are glad to have a place of their own." The thrill of seeing Blake alone and the relief that Andy was finally moving out of his house made my smile widen into a grin.

"Want to take a walk?" Blake asked. "I want to talk to you about something." Maybe he wanted to apologize for all the time he'd spent with Andy.

Suddenly, I felt like teasing. "You do know that I am a married woman, sir? And I know that you're a married man. What will our spouses say?"

"What do you say?" Blake asked Tang.

"I say get her out of here before she glues the dragon's tail to the floor. Take a walk, get some fresh air. Go!"

We walked down the path into the arboretum, an area of trees that had been donated by various service groups in town.

"So, what have you been doing these past few days? I haven't seen much of you," he said.

"That's not my fault," I snapped, then reminded myself that I didn't need to fight with Blake during the only time we had to spend together. "Sorry, I know you've been . . . obligated."

We rounded a stand of acacia trees and stepped up onto the wooden bridge over the duck pond.

"I think you'd like Andy if you got to know her. She's not as snobby as she appears, you know. She has problems and worries like everybody else."

"I don't want to talk about Andy," I said.

Blake frowned. "Actually, Andy is who I want to talk to you about," he said. "You've been acting really strange lately."

"Blake, there's something I've been meaning to tell you . . ."

A loud quacking interrupted us.

"The natives are getting restless," he observed, breaking our serious mood with a laugh. "Do you have any bread?"

I was glad to put off telling Blake what was on my mind. Now that we were finally alone together, I wasn't sure what to say to him.

"You know I always bring bread to the center, don't you?" I took a plastic bag of bread chunks out of my pocket.

"Yeah, I figured I could count on you. Hey, are those new pants? And have I seen that shirt before? There's something different about you today."

"Nice of you to finally notice," I joked, pleased that he had.

I tossed a piece of stale bread to the clamoring mass of ducks. There was a mad rush, and the biggest one got it.

"Survival of the fittest," Blake mumbled. "Here, let me toss a few to the babies over there. This oversized featherball in the front has had enough."

"I notice a lot of things, Suzanne," he continued. "For example, I noticed that you smell like honeysuckle today. I like it."

Gosh, my plan was working better than I had hoped. It seemed like things were looking up for Blake and me. Maybe I wouldn't have to say anything at all.

Unfortunately my hopes were dashed by Blake's next announcement. "Hey, I hear you guys and the Irwins are coming over to dinner tomorrow night. I guess you'll just have to put up with me for the evening. Think you can handle it?"

"I can handle you all right." I said. *It's Andrea I'd like to throw in the duck pond,* I thought.

"Race you back to the center," he challenged suddenly. Racing was our long-standing battle. Through the years we had always been evenly matched. Now, Blake was getting tall, so I had to outsmart him to win.

"No way!" I shouted, taking a head start. I put all thoughts of Andy out of my mind as I raced over the bridge, down the path, and into the pine grove. I wove in and out among the trees with Blake right behind me, but I didn't stop or turn around. We arrived, panting, at the door of the center a few moments later.

I pushed open the door, and held it for Blake. "After you, sir," I said, gesturing toward the interior.

"Thank you, madam," he replied, tipping an imaginary hat.

That's the way the rest of the morning went. We laughed a lot and teased each other and threw green cellophane scales at each other over Dino's back. But the whole time we were fooling around, the thought of dinner at the Franklins' weighed heavily on my mind. *How,* I asked myself, *was I going to get through a whole evening of Andrea Irwin?*

I didn't have much time to dwell on the matter. Dad took me shopping Saturday night, and we actually had fun. We hit just about every store in the mall, including all the nut and ice-cream stands. We came home with bags full of beautiful clothes and smiles on our faces. Mom was amazed. Carolyn pulled everything out of the bags, and of course I had to put on a fashion show.

Sunday was even more awful than I imagined it could be. Andrea charmed my parents, got to sit next to Blake, and took over the dinner table conversation with her jokes.

Everyone ignored me. Dad, Mr. Irwin, and Mrs. Franklin discussed the local elections. Mom, Mrs. Irwin, and Mr. Franklin talked about the house the Irwins planned to build while they rented the one they were in now. I didn't even have Tom to talk to. He was out on a date.

I heard Mom comment on how polite Andrea was. "Did she learn that at the private school?" she asked Mrs. Irwin.

"Oh, yes. The Academy stresses respect for your elders. Some of the children practice it better than others, though, I'm afraid."

Why had Mrs. Franklin seated me down at the opposite end of the table from Blake and Andy? I couldn't even hear their conversation, much less be a part of it.

My stomach felt as if it had a lead weight in it, and every time the laughter and the noise grew, the weight became heavier. I took a few bites of my salad, but I could hardly get them to go down. I was beginning to feel sick, and my head hurt. It seemed as if Andy never took her hand off Blake's arm.

Mom turned to me. She seemed to be talking in slow motion. "S-u-z-a-n-n-e . . . p-l-e-a-s-e . . . p-a-s-s . . . t-h-e . . . b-u-t-t-e-r."

My head was spinning. I felt as if I was going to throw up. I looked way down the table at the sea of concerned faces. A mile away, Blake and Andy finally turned and noticed that something was wrong.

"I'm not feeling well, Mom. I think I'd better go lie down."

"Yes, you do look a little peaked, dear," Mrs. Irwin commented. "Andrea was sick right before we moved. She felt woozy for days."

Dad helped me down the hall to the Franklins' guest room. "Too many lima beans, huh?" he teased, softly brushing my hair off my forehead. "Do you want a drink of water or anything? Do you want us to go home?"

"No, you just started eating," I said, closing my eyes. "I just want to lie down. Come and get me when you're ready to go."

Nine

As soon as Dad shut the door I felt better. I couldn't hear the talking and the laughter in the dining room. I couldn't see Andrea monopolizing Blake. I didn't have to pretend that I was enjoying myself.

I closed my eyes and tried to sleep, but I wasn't tired. Visions of Blake laughing at Andy's jokes filtered through my mind. I opened my eyes and looked around the room. Books were scattered everywhere. A few snapshots of Blake and me when we were little were mixed with the others over the dresser.

There was one picture of the two of us when we caught our first fish. It took both of us to hold it up for the camera. There was another one with us both waving out the window of our treehouse.

Back then all I had to worry about was Mom getting mad if I tore my jeans, or Blake and I having an equal number of peanuts to toss into the air and try to catch with our mouths.

Until the dance, I was always sure that Blake Franklin was my best friend. Now, I wondered whether or not he even liked me. And I worried that he liked Andy better than he liked me.

I clenched my fists and pounded on the pillow. Finally, I heard a knock on the door.

"Come in," I called feebly, sinking down under the covers.

"Wow, you really do look sick," Blake said, standing at the foot of my bed. "Whatever you have sure came on all of a sudden."

"That's right," I moaned. "You'd better not come too close, or you might catch it."

"Don't you think I'd already be exposed by now?" he asked, grinning.

"Oh, I don't know. You aren't around me much anymore. You're probably safe, unless Andy comes down with the same thing," I said. "In fact, why don't you go back out. I wouldn't want to keep you from having a fun evening."

"What's eating you? You've been acting weird for weeks. Are you mad at me for something? If you are, I'm sorry for whatever I've done."

"I'm not mad!" I practically shouted. Nothing, not even his sweet, apologetic expression, would get the truth out of me with Andy sitting out in the next room.

"Well, then, I'm leaving. I'm sure not going to hang around trying to cheer you up since you've decided to be a grump."

I knew I shouldn't be fighting with Blake, but I couldn't stop myself. Besides, I was sure he'd come to see me because he felt obligated, not because he wanted to. It was obvious that he'd rather be with Andy.

As if thinking of her made her appear, a knock sounded on the open door, and in walked Andy.

"I'm sorry you're sick, Suzanne. We'll miss you."

I folded my arms across my chest and glared at both of them.

"The dinner was really good," Andy told Blake, as if she couldn't sense that I didn't want her there. "I especially liked those breadsticks. Sometimes I take breadsticks to school with cheese and fruit instead of a sandwich," she rattled on. "Do you think your mom would give me the recipe?" she asked sweetly.

"No problem," Blake replied. "I'll get you the cookbook myself."

"Thanks," she gushed.

I closed my eyes again, hoping she'd take

the hint and leave.

"Well, I guess you're feeling pretty tired. I'll just go back out to the living room."

Thank goodness, I thought. Now, maybe I could start over with Blake, make up for being mad at him a minute ago. I opened my eyes. Blake was just closing the door after himself and Andy.

"Darn it!" I punched the pillow again. "Stupid. Stupid. Stupid!" I told myself. Here I was by myself, while Blake and Andy were in the living room having fun. What a dumb time to get sick. I finally went to sleep to avoid listening to them.

* * * * *

I vaguely remembered Dad waking me up and carrying me to the car. The next morning I woke up with a real fever and a sore throat. I got dressed and ready for school anyway. I wasn't going to let Andrea have another moment alone with Blake. But Mom took one look at me and sent me back to my room.

No amount of complaining and pleading did any good. I had a fever, and the doctor said I had to stay home from school for a whole week. Mom wouldn't let me take any calls or have any visitors. By Friday I was almost well, and I was completely bored.

"I feel 100 percent better, Mom. May I please go to school today?" I asked at breakfast.

She felt my head. She looked at my eyes. "I'm sure you're fine, but let's give it one more day, shall we? We don't want you to have a relapse."

"What about the trial run on our raft tomorrow?" I asked softly. "If I stay home today, may I please go out tomorrow?"

"In the water?" she asked. "I don't know if that's a good idea."

"I'll be careful. I won't get wet."

She looked at me disbelievingly.

"I'll take an extra set of warm clothes and a hair dryer," I added quickly.

"I'm sure it will be all right, Nancy," Dad said, coming into the room carrying Carolyn. "She could probably even go to school today."

I nodded my head up and down vigorously.

"No," Mom said firmly. "If you're feeling energetic today, you can catch up on your homework. Tiffany brought it by yesterday afternoon."

* * * * *

I spent the day writing reports and doing

math. I did everything Mom told me to do. I played blocks and trains with Carolyn. I was a perfect child.

The next morning I was pronounced fit, and I was given permission to go rafting.

"Remember, try not to get too tired," Mom warned.

"Don't worry, Mom. I won't overdo. Anyway, I'm coming home early. Tang and I have lost a whole week of working on our project. It's a good thing we did most of it last weekend. All we have left to work on is the class presentation."

"Why don't you bring the gang here for lunch?" Dad suggested.

"Okay, I will," I said, sailing out the door, and practically running all the way to the rec center. I hoped everybody hadn't left without me, still expecting me to be sick.

Dino's head was just emerging from the double doors at the back of the center as I rounded the corner. "Here, let me help," I offered, tossing my pack of extra clothes on a nearby bench.

"Lucky thing the dock is only a few yards away," Joyce said, straining to keep her corner up. I hurried to get in between Tiff and Joyce to help hold up the back end. Dino's tail swung lazily above my head.

"Wow, he looks great. I'm sorry I wasn't able to help finish him."

"We're just glad you're here for the maiden voyage," Tiff remarked. "How are you feeling?"

"Fine. I was a wreck for a few days, though."

We reached the water's edge, walked out into the shallows, and slowly lowered the raft until it was floating.

Suddenly we heard a shout from the opposite side as Blake grabbed the tilting neck. "It's too front heavy," he said.

"Maybe we can balance the weight by putting the guys in the back and the girls on the sides," I suggested.

I climbed on the right side with Andy in front of me. Joyce and Tiffany took the left side. Blake stood behind me, Mac was behind Joyce, and Tang took the tail. For a few minutes Dino tipped first to one side, then the other. Finally he settled upright.

"Fantastic!" Tang shouted. "Let's take her around the inlet where the current can't catch us. Does everybody have a paddle?"

"Yes!" we all shouted back.

"Cast off!" Tang signaled.

Paddles slapped the water, and Tang started calling out, "Stroke, stroke." But no one was paying attention, least of all Andy.

I dug my paddle in, hoping to make up for her inept strokes. "Haven't you ever rowed a boat before? You have to dig in, not slap the water. Do it like this." I showed her.

Andy slapped again, and I got a mouthful of water. I tried a second time. "Like this," I said, gracefully dipping my paddle into the calm water and pulling it backward slowly.

This time Andy dug the paddle too deep into the water and almost lost it. She yanked so hard to get it back up, that once again I ended up drenched.

By this time the raft was going around in circles, since the group on the other side wasn't having any problem stroking in unison.

"Switch with Andy, Suzanne," Blake said, laughing. "I'll show her how to paddle."

"Enjoy your bath, Blake," I retorted, easing around Andy into the front position. *Boy,* I thought angrily, *even her incompetence works to her advantage.*

I tried to ignore Blake as he taught Andy how to paddle. "Now look," he said, taking her hands and placing them on the paddle. "Reach down like this. Barely slice the water. Not so deep. Easy. That's right. Now, pull back steadily and lift the paddle out of the water."

I didn't look back to see his arms around her helping her with the paddle. Instead I slapped my paddle into the water hard, and soaked them. I glanced over my shoulder. "Oh, sorry," I apologized. "My paddle slipped."

After that things went from bad to worse. Andy fell overboard, and Blake had to save her. She didn't have any dry clothes, so Blake offered her the extra ones he'd brought. Then before I could invite everyone over to my house for lunch, Andy managed to produce a picnic basket filled with sandwiches and soft drinks.

I couldn't believe the way the rest of the group hung on her every word. I didn't want to hear a description of the plans for her family's new house, or about their difficulty in finding a maid. I didn't want to hear about all the letters she was getting from her friends back East who missed her. Andrea Irwin was just too good to be true. There had to be something about her that wasn't perfect, but I couldn't figure out what it was.

No one noticed when I got up to leave. They were all busy eating and listening to Andy. Halfway home, the tears came. Wiping them away did no good at all.

At home I didn't have much trouble convincing my parents that I wanted to rest before Tang came over. They didn't say a word about lunch.

Once I was safely in my room, I let the tears

come again. Silently I sobbed into my pillow. Why had Andy moved back to town? Why couldn't things be the way they used to be with Blake and me?

Somehow I would have to make it happen.

I rested for a while, then finally went to the bathroom to wash my face. I put on a dash of fresh makeup to cover my red eyes.

Tang arrived right on schedule. He didn't say anything about my appearance when he arrived. He didn't say anything about my disappearance from the center either. Tang was a good friend.

"I had an idea for our oral report," I told him when we had settled ourselves at the dining room table. I pulled out some poster board and my craft box that was filled with everything—construction paper, marking pens, glue, glitter—you name it. "Let's hit them with visual effects. Remember how Mr. Boxwell is always holding up a picture to prove his point?"

"I know, visual aids," Tang said. Then he quoted our teacher, "Visual aids are a way of graphically illustrating your point of view to the audience. One picture is worth a thousand words, but that doesn't mean you can get out of writing the report by showing a picture."

I had to laugh. "Do you memorize everything he says?"

"It's pretty hard to avoid it when Boxy repeats himself at least six times in a row." Tang laughed, too.

We set to work cutting out magazine pictures of children's faces and glued them on one sheet of poster board to represent our six kids. Then we wrote out our budget in bold black letters on another piece of poster board.

Suddenly Tang jumped up, waving his markers and dancing around in a circle. "I've got it! I've got it!" he yelled. "It's something that no one else will think of. Let's write a play about how we coped with one of the complications we thought up. I think the time when I get my ego bent out of shape when you tell me you've landed a good job would make the best scene."

"Great idea, Tang."

"I'm not such a bad husband after all, huh? Even if I was second choice?"

I smiled, thinking about how Tang always made me laugh. I'd had more fun with Tang since I started liking Blake than I had with Blake. Life was sure mixed up.

As soon as we finished the posters, we began writing the play. Actually, it was more like a short skit. We planned what we'd wear and what props we'd need. I was sure our skit idea would be a big hit.

Ten

BOXY had really outdone himself this time. On Monday morning, we walked into our classroom to find a flowered arch hung over the doorway and white baskets filled with flowers in every corner. The smell of carnations was everywhere. It was a nice change from the odor of chalk dust and floor polish.

"What did you do? Rob a wedding?" Tạng asked as we took our seats.

"Close," Mr. Boxwell admitted. "My niece got married on Saturday. I just appropriated the goods. I hope you're all prepared," he added on a more serious note. "I will not be calling on you in alphabetical order, so your team could be asked to give your report at any time. If you're not prepared the day I call on you, your grade will automatically drop one letter. Understood?"

We all nodded our heads. We were used to

Mr. Boxwell. "Be prepared, or else," was his motto.

"I hope we get called on today," I whispered to Tang. "I'm really excited about our skit, and I want us to be one of the first groups, in case another team had the same idea."

He gave me a thumbs-up sign. I glanced over at Blake and Andy. They had their heads together whispering about something. I promised myself that I wasn't going to let them get to me.

Karen and Leroy were called first. Karen wrote their budget on the board while Leroy read from behind the podium. I stifled a yawn.

At the end of their presentation, Boxy granted them a divorce.

"I wouldn't want to stay in a marriage that dull, either," Tang whispered to me.

Tiffany and Mike were called next. Their presentation was a little more lively. Mike came up to the front wearing a pilot's hat and carrying his saxophone. As Tiffany joined him, he played notes that mimicked her steps. She wore a pilot's hat, too, and she held her notepad like a steering wheel, pretending she was flying an airplane.

Suddenly Mike let out a loud squeak on the sax. Then he threw off his hat and started playing low, sad notes. Tiffany patted her stomach. Then she told the class how wonderful things had been until Mike lost his job and she got pregnant.

"We decided that I would continue flying as long as the doctor would let me," Tiffany explained. "Meanwhile, Mike would put in his application at other airlines and at private flight training schools. By the time I needed to stop working, Mike would have another job. After the baby was a year old, I planned to start flying again."

"What if Mike couldn't get a job immediately?" Boxy asked.

"We set aside some money for just that possibility, because both of us knew how difficult the air industry can be. Also, my parents told us we could move in with them until we got on our feet again. They also offered to lend us some money," Mike said.

After Mike and Tiffany finished their report and the class asked a few more questions, Boxy asked, "Do you still want to be married to this person?"

Both Tiffany and Mike said yes.

Mr. Boxwell reached dramatically into the bowl with our names in it. Out of the corner of my eye I saw Andrea squirm nervously.

Pick us, pick us, I wished silently. Each pair had 10 minutes to give their presentations. We only had time for two more couples. I really wanted to go today.

"Will the Dalmases please come forward?" Boxy boomed, banging his gavel on the bench.

"This is it, Mrs. Dalmas," Tang whispered.

"That's Ms. Doyle to you, buster. I thought we'd been all through the name change bit," I replied, loud enough for the class to hear me. We went right into our skit.

"Just because you've gotten yourself a high-powered job doesn't mean you're not married anymore," Tang snapped, affecting a hurt pose.

"Your ego simply can't handle the fact that I spent 15 years out of career circulation, but I was able to jump right back in. Just think. If your company hadn't folded, we never would have found out how much I've been missing by staying home with the six kids," I replied.

"My company didn't fold because of me!" Tang said, raising his voice. "I'm the best darn software designer ABTEC ever had. If it hadn't been for me, ABTEC would have gone under long ago."

"So why do you begrudge me *my* moment of success?" I asked. "Besides, you have the perfect opportunity to stay home and get to know your children and try out your wonderful management skills on running a household."

"Well, you're right. Being at home is a full-time job. I thought I'd be much more organized than you were. I figured I'd have everything running smoothly and be able to play golf every day."

"Things didn't work out quite the way you planned, did they?" I remarked sarcastically.

"Well, if you made more money, life would be easier. We can't even afford a part-time maid anymore."

"Take a look at this check stub." I waved a small piece of paper under his nose. "My income is almost identical to what yours was. It's your spending habits that are breaking us."

We broke from our skit for a moment to show the class the two posters we'd made to illustrate the difference in the family's spending patterns when Tang was working and when I was working. Our incomes were about the same, but Tang tended to overspend on non-essentials and impulse items. Then we showed a third chart that we worked out together after we realized the mistakes we were making.

Tang began to read to the class. "After Suzanne and I resolved the problem of money management, we worked out a household management routine that left me with more free time. After I stopped spending money on junk, we were able to save enough to hire a baby-sitter two mornings per week to give me a chance to get out."

I faced the class. "You see, once the budget and the matters of child care and household chores were worked out, life around the Dalmas/Doyle house became much easier. But Tang still wasn't happy."

Tang fell back into our skit. "Managing the house is fulfilling, Suzanne, but I need to work. I don't know what to do, though. My education and experience make me over-qualified for anything available in this town. And, I don't want to move to the city. I enjoy the space and the nonpolluted air."

I sat down next to Tang. "As I see it you have two choices. You can continue to stay home while I work, or you can start your own business."

Tang once again addressed the class. "Starting my own business was the best thing that ever happened to me. I built an office onto the back of our home, worked while the kids were at school, and sold my software packages directly to the computer manufacturers."

"Sounds great!" Leroy quipped. "But, when do you have time for Suzanne?"

"Good question," Tang said, putting his arm around me. "Suzanne and I realized that our relationship was more important than our jobs. We finally hired a live-in sitter who watches the kids in the evenings while we go to the health spa, or on the weekends when we sail away on our yacht."

Everyone laughed except Blake. He had a funny expression on his face.

"Would you stay married to this person?" Mr. Boxwell finally asked. "I seem to remember that there was some doubt about the outcome of the relationship from the beginning."

Tang spoke first. "We found that overcoming all the obstacles placed in front of us made our relationship stronger than ever. In fact, adversity bred ingenuity."

"And what's that supposed to mean in English?" someone called.

Tang laughed. "No pain, no gain," he replied. "And in answer to your question, Mr. Boxwell, we've decided to stay married."

"That's right," I said sincerely. "Working out our problems was half the fun," I added.

"All right. Good job. You can take your seats."

There was a rousing cheer from the class and a round of hand-clapping. I smiled at Tang. Giving this report had really been fun.

"We have time for one more couple," Mr. Boxwell said, returning to his judgelike voice.

"And the next lucky couple is . . . " he dug into the bowl. "Blake Franklin and Andrea Irwin."

Andrea and Blake went to the front of the room. Blake began by showing the class a beautifully drawn sketch of a home in the suburbs with a family working in the garden. Overhead in black lettering the caption read, "The Perfect Family." I knew Andy had drawn the picture.

"Andy and I had everything. We owned our own business, a chain of fast food restaurants across the western United States. During the first few years of our marriage, we bought everything we wanted—cars, boats, a home in town, a home in the country, a ski chalet in the mountains. Our children went to the best private schools. We had a succession of nannies to maintain order around the house, and we hired a managerial group to take care of our finances."

Andy held up another picture of the same family. This time they were seated around a table, talking to each other.

"Unfortunately," Blake went on, "life isn't like a storybook. Both of us were workaholics. We rarely saw our children, and the family finally went into therapy.

Gosh, I thought, *their report is almost the exact scenario I had suggested at lunch the day this project was assigned. How dare they use my ideas?* I glared at Andy, but she wasn't paying attention. She was holding the picture up in front of her face and biting her nails.

Good, I thought. *I hope she feels really embarrassed.*

She held up another picture. This one was of two teenage children lounging in front of the television set. Their clothes were dirty, and the couch was littered with garbage.

"Our children became disillusioned with life," Blake continued. "They got in with the wrong crowd . . ."

"They must take after their parents," one boy jeered good-naturedly from the back of the room.

Blake laughed. "Actually, I thought I saw them hanging around with you, Ernie," was his quick comeback.

"Excuse me," Mr. Boxwell interrupted. "The grade is 50 percent content and 50 percent participation. That means both partners must share the written and oral parts of the presentation. Are you planning on speaking, Andrea?"

"Oh, sure, we were just coming to that part," Blake said quickly. He turned to Andy and whispered something to her that we couldn't hear.

"They say a picture's worth a thousand words, but I don't hear anything," Tang said in a poor imitation of Boxy's voice.

Andy took the note cards. She cleared her throat as Blake held up the picture of the drugged-out kids.

"How about a song, Andy?" Leroy prompted.

"Uh, like Blake said, they got in with a bad crowd," she repeated, then looked at the notes. "They—uh—started getting suspended from school. My brother—I mean—son almost ki—kil—killed someone in a car accident. Then Blake walked out on the family."

I looked around at the faces in the classroom. Some were still chuckling over Leroy's remark about having Andy sing a song. But most were watching Andy. From the look on her face, you'd have thought this was real, not just an oral report.

"How did you solve the problems?" Mr. Boxwell asked.

"We moved and started fresh in a new community," Blake said.

"Are there any questions?" Mr. Boxwell asked the class, clearly not satisfied with Blake's answer.

"I have a question," I spoke up. "Wasn't moving to a new town kind of like running away from your problems?"

"Would you like me to answer that, Andy?" Blake offered.

"No, I will." There were tears in her eyes when she faced me. *Great act,* I thought. *She's really good.*

"We didn't just run away," she told me. "We try to work less now and have more family time. We're still in therapy. It may not be perfect yet, but at least my dad—I mean Blake—is back home and trying to keep the family together."

"So long as your *son* stays away from the wrong crowd," I joked, trying to loosen her up a bit and make her stop stuttering and giving Blake a bad grade.

But Andy wasn't laughing. In fact, she was crying.

"Andy," I said, "it was just a joke . . ."

Blake's eyes met mine. "You've really done it this time," was all he said before he slowly led Andy out of the room.

Eleven

As I stood there watching Blake lead Andy away, a million things went through my mind. Was Andy's real family like the family she described in her report? Was Tom in trouble at school? Did her family really go to counseling?

I didn't know the answers, but I knew that I had to fix something fast. If what Andy said was true, I'd been wrong about her all along. Maybe Blake really had been helping her adjust. I had to apologize.

I ran out into the hall, but Blake and Andy were nowhere to be seen. I checked the girls' bathroom, the cafeteria, the office, and the picnic tables outside. There was no sign of them.

The bell rang for lunch just as I reached my locker. I pulled my books out, grabbed my jacket, and headed out to the parking lot. I ran over to Blake's house.

Blake wasn't home, and Mrs. Franklin looked at me as if I were nuts, but she gave me Andy's new address anyway. I assured her that everything was all right and asked if she'd call my parents to tell them where I was. I planned to explain everything when I got home.

I jogged all the way to Andrea's house. I rang the doorbell, but no one answered.

"Andrea! Are you in there?" I called loudly. "It's Suzanne. Please open the door."

I rang the bell again and pounded on the door. Finally, I heard footsteps inside.

"What do you want?" she said softly through the door. I could tell she was still crying.

"I want to talk with you. May I come in?"

"Blake's not here," she said, opening the door a crack.

That was a relief. I didn't think I could face both of them at once. "I came to talk to you, not Blake."

She opened the door. "Okay."

We sat down on the couch in the living room. I couldn't help but notice all the fancy, expensive-looking paintings hanging around. Ceramic vases sat on all the tables, and a brass clock with a glass dome was the center-piece for the coffee table.

"Boy, my little sister would destroy this place in minutes," I said, trying to open the conversation.

"Tom and I are old enough to know better," she replied.

"I know. It was just a dumb comment. My sister isn't what I came to talk to you about. I came to say I'm sorry about what I said in class. I didn't mean to hurt your feelings."

"Well, you did. You've done nothing but hurt my feelings since I moved here. All I've done was try to be friends."

Her self-pitying attitude was too much. "A friend wouldn't try to take away a friend's boyfriend," I stated hotly. "You've been after Blake since the moment you set foot here in Parker."

"I have not! Besides, Blake isn't your boyfriend." Andy was mad now, too. Her tears had stopped, and so had her sweet act. "Blake is just your friend. Can't he be my friend, too?"

"Well, he would have been my boyfriend if you hadn't come along. Blake and I have been best friends our whole lives. Now, suddenly he's spending all his time with you."

She sighed, slumping her shoulders. She looked like she might cry again. "Blake has been nice to me, and he offered to help me . . . adjust."

"Adjust, my foot," I growled. "I've watched you since you moved here. You don't have any problems making friends. That charm of yours is like a faucet. Whenever you need it you just turn it on." Then I started mimicking her. "Your casserole is delicious, Mrs. Franklin. I'd love to have the recipe." "I just can't seem to get the knack of it, Blake. Please teach me to row." "Oh, yes, Mr. Boxwell, I love your class. You're the most interesting teacher I've ever had."

"What is your problem?" I demanded. "Who is the real Andrea, anyway?" I continued sarcastically. I was no longer sorry for what I'd said in class. As far as I could tell, her crying was just another piece of acting to get attention.

She sniffed. "I don't know who the real Andrea is anymore. Everything I said today in class is true. My family is a mess. I never know whether my dad is coming home or not. My brother is starting to bring home weird friends again. And I don't have anyone to talk to except Blake."

"What about all your friends back East, the ones you get letters from all the time?"

"I lied. I didn't have any friends when we moved, because the whole school knew about our problems. I didn't tell anyone here except

Blake, because I knew no one would like me if they knew about my family."

She broke down crying again, and I stared at her bent head.

"Is that the truth?" I asked, knowing that it was.

She nodded, still sobbing into her hands.

"Oh," I said, stunned. "Now I really am sorry for the way I've been treating you." I handed her a tissue. "Then you're really not trying to take Blake away from me?" I asked, still wanting reassurance.

"Honest, I'm not."

The room grew silent as Andy slowly stopped crying. I watched the pendulum swing back and forth on a beautiful wall clock.

Andy blew her nose one last time and then looked at me squarely.

"You know, you were right about all the acts I put on. I had to. I found out a long time ago that people don't ask so many questions when I put on a big smile and shower them with compliments."

"But isn't it better to talk about your feelings than to hide them? That's what my mother always says."

She laughed a little at that. "I don't get much chance to talk. My parents are always too busy fighting about their lives. And my brother is busy fighting about getting his privileges back, now that he's supposedly fixed his attitude," Andy said.

"Why don't you make them listen to you?"

"Because every time I mention that I'm having a hard time, my parents tell me what a great daughter I am. They're proud that I was a cheerleader, a student council member, and that I always attend the community events that they're involved in. They say, 'Thank goodness we never have any problems with you, Andy, because Tom is about all we can handle right now.' "

"Sounds like Tom can be a brat. He keeps your parents so busy that they don't have any time left over for you."

"Just like the report said," she remarked.

"I'm surprised you were able to give it at all," I told her.

"I couldn't, remember? I ran out of the room. Now what will everybody think of me?"

"Don't worry about it," I said. "Just be yourself. Nobody cares whether or not you go to therapy, especially not our gang. You can't drop out of sight now, you know. We need you for the race next Saturday. And besides, I'd like for us to become friends."

"Do you really think we could be friends?" she asked hesitantly.

"I'd like to try," I said.

"Well, if you want me for a friend, first you have to listen to some friendly advice. You're really blowing it with Blake."

"I know I am. I was so jealous of you I couldn't see straight. I don't know how I can fix it with Blake," I moaned. "He trusted me, and I let him down."

"Oh, it's not that bad," she told me. "You were jealous. He should be flattered."

"I don't know what to say to him." I shook my head. "It's funny. Blake and I have always told each other everything since we were kids. Suddenly we're keeping secrets from each other and saying terrible things to each other. The look he gave me in class today was awful."

"If you're interested in my opinion, I think you should talk to him. You've been friends too long to let something like this get in the way. Besides," she added, "I'd never forgive myself if you two stopped being friends because of me."

I grinned at her in spite of myself. "You're probably right. Tell you what. I'll talk to Blake if you talk to your parents."

She smiled. "What have we got to lose?"

Twelve

DURING the rest of the week I tried to talk to Blake, but I could never find an opportunity. I called him twice, but he wouldn't come to the phone.

At school I tried to show him that Andy and I were becoming friends. Normally I would have had a chance to see him on the way home from school, but I had to stay in detention for cutting class on Monday. Andy had to stay for detention, too. We learned a lot about each other by passing notes during our hour of silence each day for the rest of the week.

"I don't know what to do," I told Andy on Friday. "Every time I try to talk to him, he manages to avoid me. He hasn't even been to the center to help us put the final touches on the float."

"I know. I've never seen anybody be so stubborn. He won't even talk to me. I guess he figures I'm the one who caused the problem in the first place by swearing him to secrecy about my family situation," she replied. "Well, he can't avoid us tomorrow at the race. He *has* to be there."

"I hope you're right."

"I'll help you. We'll get him to listen somehow."

"At least the rest of the group isn't mad at me," I said. I had apologized to each one of them individually during the week for letting my jealousy get in the way of being nice to my friends.

I remembered that conversation with Andy as I got dressed the next morning. Despite my problems with Blake, I was looking forward to the race. We'd all worked so hard to prepare for it. Friday night we'd put the final touches on Dino—a wreath of flowers for his big green head and a brightly-colored flag for his tail. The fish in his mouth dangled from a big brass-colored fishhook in honor of the restaurant's name. No one was going to miss us floating down the river.

"The Brass Fishhook provides breakfast for the entrants," I explained to my parents a few minutes later in the kitchen, so I'll get going right away. The gang is meeting at the center to carry Dino down to the river."

"Good luck, honey." Mom kissed me on the cheek. "We'll follow you along the route as best we can from shore, and meet you at the finish line."

"Dino, Dino," Carolyn chanted. "Dino, me go."

"Sorry, sweetie, not this time," I had to tell her. "But I'll lift you onto his back when we're done, okay?"

"We'll let her wade at the shore. She'll forget all about riding the dragon," Dad reassured me.

"See you guys later—in the winner's circle," I added on my way out the door.

I started to get really excited as I approached the recreation center. It seemed like thousands of people were running around, pulling and tugging on their rafts. Last minute instructions filled the air, punctuated by cries of alarm and moans of distress.

In contrast to that, I found Dino sitting quietly in the corner, with just Blake checking to make sure all the ropes were tight.

"Hi," I said hesitantly. "Can we talk?"

"Now isn't a very good time, Suzanne," he said, still facing the dragon.

"Andy and I have become friends," I told him. "That's what you wanted, isn't it?"

"Why do you care about my opinion? You

haven't listened to a word I've said for weeks."

"I know, and I'm sorry. Will you forgive me?"

"I'll think about it," was all he said.

Just then, the rest of the gang arrived. Andy gave me a questioning look. I shook my head.

"Can we talk about this after the race?" I asked Blake.

Blake stared at me for a long time before answering. I didn't know what to do, so I just met his gaze.

"Yes," he said finally.

I didn't even have time for a sigh of relief before Tang began ordering us to get Dino moving down to the water. "We only have 30 minutes to go. Let's get this reptile to the starting line."

"That's right," I said with more enthusiasm than I had felt in days. "We don't want to miss the starting whistle."

"I don't want to miss breakfast," Mac said.

All the way to the river we shouted encouragement to everyone we passed. Dino was pretty heavy, even with seven of us lifting him. After we'd finally reached the river's edge, I launched into my pep talk. Andy was right beside me.

"I know we can keep Dino afloat for a mile," I said. "We just have to keep our wits about us. Think balance! Think steady!"

"Think teamwork!" Andy chimed in.

Tang reached around and bobbed Dino's head up and down. "Even Dino agrees," he informed us.

"You fixed it so it tips!" I exclaimed. "Wow, that's fantastic!"

Tang beamed. "We did it the week you were sick. Nice surprise, huh?"

"I'm definitely impressed."

"Can we eat now and be impressed later?" Mac suggested. "I'm starving."

The restaurant was crowded with participants, but there was plenty of food for everyone. We had just finished wolfing down rolls and fruit when the announcement blared over the loudspeaker. "Take your positions. We're ready to begin."

To Dino's right was a pirate ship. To the left was a giant air-filled hot dog.

"Does everyone have a life jacket on?" Tiffany asked.

"Check," we said one by one.

Andy took up her position behind me, gripping her oar firmly. Tiffany and Joyce climbed on the other side. Carefully, the guys slid the huge creature into the water to await the starting signal.

A second later a loud whistle blew. "Go!" we

shouted above the din of voices, splashing, and laughter.

Tang, Mac, and Blake pushed with all their might until the bottom was too deep. Together, they jumped on, and we immediately started paddling.

We were surrounded by other entrants. I saw several log rafts, a couple of contraptions that resembled spaceships, and a wide assortment of floating junkpiles that didn't resemble anything.

We weren't afloat for more than a few minutes before several of the rafts around us began to sink. The crew of the spaceship next to us jumped off yelling. "Eject! Eject!" as their craft did a nosedive.

"I can see the headlines in the paper tomorrow," Tang quipped. "Spaceship lands in the Colorado River. Area evacuated."

"Whoops! There goes the pirate ship," Mac said, pointing to the listing frigate. "Watch out, it's going to hit us."

Andy, Blake, and I paddled with all our might to avoid a crash. We watched the skull and crossbones flutter and sink beneath the surface.

"I hope we make it," Tiffany said.

"Dino's holding up pretty well," Blake remarked. "We'll make it."

I smiled. "I don't care if we win. I just hope we get there in one piece."

"We still have the rapids to get past," Mac said ominously. He patted Dino's tail. "Come on, boy. You can do it."

I looked over at Blake. I hoped he could see that Andy and I were really becoming friends now.

We sailed along smoothly, rounded a bend, and saw the restaurant in the distance. "Rapids coming up," Tiffany announced. "Steady as she goes, sailors."

The rapids right before the end of the race route weren't bad if you were in a rubber raft or a kayak, but on Dino, every little ripple seemed like a mountain.

"Whoa!" I said as the raft tipped first one way and then the other. "There's a rock ahead on the right," I yelled. "Dig in! Dig in!"

We rowed as hard as we could, pulling back on our paddles to the limit, but Dino's back corner hit the rock anyway. Blake fell off, and when he did, the whole raft tilted to the left.

"Are you all right?" I yelled back to Blake, who was being tossed along behind us.

"I'm fine," he yelled back. "Keep going."

"Take Blake's place on the back corner," Mac called to Tang. "Otherwise we're going to tip."

As he said that we heard a huge crack. Then dino's tail broke loose. Tang grabbed the tail, but couldn't move to the back corner and hold onto the tail at the same time.

"We're going over," Tiffany shouted above the roar of the water.

"No, we're not." Andy grabbed my arm and said, "Lean way out like they do on sailboats. I may not be able to paddle, but I know how to keep a catamaran upright."

I did as she instructed. The extra leverage we got by leaning out righted the raft.

"Can you climb back on?" Tang asked Blake, who was now swimming just behind the raft.

"I can't until you clear the rapids."

We somehow managed to hold on. "That was the longest minute of my life," I gasped when we finally popped out of the rough water and shot toward the restaurant. I looked around to find that we were right behind the lead raft, a pontoon design with small sails stretched along both sides.

"Hey, you guys, we're almost there, and we're in second place."

"Hurry up and climb on, Blake. We could win this." Joyce said.

We helped Blake back onto the raft, and he just lay for a second, exhausted.

"Enjoy your swim?" I teased.

"Better watch it. I'll toss you in next," he threatened.

I laughed. That sounded like the old Blake.

"Come on, you two. Stop yapping and start paddling," Andy complained from between us.

Tang called out, "Stroke, stroke, stroke," until we got into rhythm. "We're gaining on them," he said.

That was probably because the other raft only had two people paddling.

On shore, the crowd started cheering. I saw my family standing at the finish line waving to us.

"Faster!" "Harder!" "Keep it steady!" "We're going to make it!" We kept up a continuous chatter as we pulled on our paddles with all our might.

We were neck and neck, or should I say neck and bow, when we crossed the finish line. I looked up to see Tang working the mechanism to flap the wings and raise Dino's head up and down for the cameras.

I didn't know whether we had won or not, I was just excited that we'd finished in almost one piece. We waded out onto shore to receive the congratulatory hugs of parents, friends, and onlookers. I looked back to see the rest of the rafts floating, struggling, or limping in. It was quite a collection, and I was proud to be part of it.

Suddenly a man in a suit and captain's cap was standing in front of us. "Congratulations," he said. "Not only did you win the Anything That Floats race by a nose, but you've also won an additional prize for best animated craft."

"Was that one of the categories?" Mac asked.

"No. I just made it up in honor of our first moving float."

"We did it! We did it!" We all jumped up and down, hugging each other and Dino.

When we finally settled down a bit, the man introduced himself as Mr. Zucherman, the owner of The Brass Fishhook. He handed us a trophy and a gift certificate for 12 dinners for seven, one per month.

Flashbulbs started snapping and reporters surrounded us to write down our names. We had to go up on a platform to wave to the crowd.

As we came down off the stage, Blake grabbed me by the arms. "Now it's your turn," he informed me.

Before I could ask, "My turn for what?" he was walking me toward the river's edge.

He threw me in the water with a loud splash.

In less than a minute almost everyone on the beach was in the water with us, having a gigantic water fight.

I splashed Blake, and I splashed Andy. She splashed me back. Then we both turned on Blake, drenching him with our onslaught.

"I talked to my parents," Andy said between splashes.

We turned around and began aiming sheets of water backward to avoid getting our faces wet.

"What did they say?"

"You were right. They agreed that they'd probably been pushing me too hard. They called the counselor and arranged for me to have a few private sessions. Dad told me not to worry. He's not going to leave again. He's going to stick it out and make the family work somehow."

"That's great," I said. "Have you noticed that we're not getting splashed anymore?"

"I wonder why?" she asked suspiciously.

"I suppose we'd better turn around and find out."

"Ready? One . . . two . . . three . . ." We both spun around at once, ready to meet Blake's next attack. But, it wasn't just Blake. Tang, Joyce, Mac, and Tiffany were on either side of Blake. The second we turned around, they all slammed a huge fountain of water directly at us.

The force knocked us down. We came up sputtering and laughing. "I give," Andy said, holding up her hands in surrender.

"Me, too," I threw my hands in the air also.

"Food, anyone?" Mr. Zucherman announced over another loudspeaker.

Blake came up beside me. "Are you hungry, Suzanne?"

I smiled a watery smile. "Starved. How about you, Andy?" I said, pulling her over to join us.

"I think I swallowed the whole river," she said, coughing. "But, I'm willing to wash it down with some food."

Later, after we'd eaten, Blake took me aside. We walked along the shore counting the rafts that had finished. "You really have become friends with Andy, haven't you?" he said when we reached the end of the cove. He seemed amazed.

"Yes, but it would have been easier if you'd told me the whole situation from the beginning," I informed him. "But that was still no excuse for the way I acted. I'm sorry. I was way out of line."

"She asked me not to tell anyone. She needed a friend in the worst way. I still don't understand why you were so down on her, though."

I took a deep breath and decided to be honest. "You and I have been so close for so long. I had this stupid idea that she was taking you away from me. I felt left out."

"You probably had reason to feel that way. I was pretty caught up in Andy's problems."

"Are we still friends, Blake?"

He took my hand in his and held it for a moment. "More than just friends, I hope."

I hoped so, too.

"Race you back to the restaurant," he said.

"You're on!" I shouted, taking off for a head start.

Blake stuck out his foot and tripped me. He jumped over me as I was picking myself up and ran like the wind toward the crowd.

"Cheater!" I screamed at his back, running hard to catch up. "Wait till I get my hands on you! Watch out, Blake," I said a second later as I came abreast of him. "Your shoe's untied."

He looked down at his bare feet as I zoomed past.

I laughed over my shoulder. "Gotcha!"

About the Author

CINDY SAVAGE lives in a big rambling house on a tiny farm in northern California with her husband, Greg, her three birth children, and an assortment of foster children.

She published her first poem in a local newspaper when she was six years old, and soon after got hooked on reading and writing. After college she taught bilingual Spanish/English preschool, then took a break to have her own children. Now she stays home with her kids and writes magazine articles and books for children and young adults.

In between writing and acting as chauffeur to a very active family, she reads, does needlework, bakes bread, and tends the garden.

Traveling has always been one of her favorite hobbies. As a child she crossed the United States many times with her parents, visiting Canada and Mexico along the way. Now she takes shorter trips to the ocean and the mountains to get recharged. She gets her inspiration to write from the places she visits and the people she meets.